Disney · PIXAR

INSIDE OUT

Sadness
Saves the Day!

randomhousekids.com

ISBN 978-0-7364-3637-3 (trade) — ISBN 978-0-7364-8228-8 (lib. bdg.)

Printed in the United States of America

10 9 8 7 6 5 4 3 2 1

Disney · PIXAR
INSIDE OUT

Sadness Saves the Day!

By Tracey West

Illustrated by the Disney Storybook Art Team

Random House 🏠 New York

Welcome to Headquarters!

Meet the Five Emotions who live inside Riley's mind: Joy, Sadness, Anger, Disgust, and Fear. They help Riley make decisions every day.

A few months ago, Riley moved from Minnesota to San Francisco. Although things were rocky at first, Riley has made some new friends and she's really happy now. Things are going pretty smoothly . . .

. . . until one day, Sadness accidentally gets whisked back to the Mind World. How will Riley cope without Sadness when a new girl arrives at school? And can Sadness get back to Headquarters without Joy to help her this time? The answer is up to you, because in this book, *you* decide the ending!

"What's all this racket?" Anger fumes, stomping across the floor of the bedroom in Headquarters.

It's nighttime, and twelve-year-old Riley is sound asleep. But inside her mind, there's a lot going on.

Downstairs, three Mind Workers are tinkering with the console, the control panel that Riley's Five Emotions use to help her make decisions. The Mind Workers don't normally come to Headquarters, but every once in a while, the console needs a little upkeep. Their tools are clinking and clanking as they work.

Disgust walks up to Anger, yawning. Some of her green hair is out of place.

"How is a girl supposed to get her beauty sleep with all this noise?" she asks.

"Beauty sleep, ugly sleep, I don't care what kind of sleep it is," says Anger. "I just want to sleep!"

Fear wakes with a start. "Fire! Emergency! Earthquake!" he yells.

Sadness is awake now, too. "It's fine. It's just some Mind Workers fixing the console," she assures him. "I might as well see how they're doing. I'll never go back to sleep now."

She changes out of her pajamas into her favorite comfy sweater. Then she walks down to the Control Room.

The three Mind Workers are hard at work. They all look pretty much alike. Each one has a round body, big eyes, a wide mouth, and skinny arms and legs. Only some have hair, though, and they come in different colors. These three are wearing construction helmets.

Behind the console, Joy is sitting in a chair and watching a big screen. Each night, one

of the Emotions stays awake to go on Dream Duty. Tonight it's Joy's turn.

"Won't all this noise wake up Riley?" Sadness asks Joy.

"Riley's fine!" Joy replies, glowing with golden energy. "She's having another nice dream. She's been so happy here in San Francisco these last few weeks."

Sadness adjusts her big round eyeglasses and looks at the dream on the screen. A unicorn with a rainbow-colored mane and tail is

galloping through a sunny field of flowers.

"Things are good now, but that won't last forever," says Sadness. "Nothing does."

"But Riley's made new friends, and her new hockey team is doing great," counters Joy.

"They lost their last game," Sadness reminds her.

"And then they went out for frozen yogurt and Riley put too many sprinkles on hers, and Sam said it was like a rainbow throwing up and everyone laughed and laughed. Remember that? That was so much fun," Joy says.

"I guess," Sadness replies.

"Aw, come on, of course it was fun!" Joy insists. "Everything's going really well! Now let's enjoy this awesome dream."

Sadness sulks over to the Mind Workers and watches them work on the console.

"Shouldn't that cable go in the red port?" Sadness asks an orange Mind Worker.

"Step back, young lady," he snaps. "This is delicate business."

"I can help," Sadness replies. "I've read every manual there is about the Mind World."

"Well, isn't that nice?" says the orange Mind Worker, patting her on the head like she's a little kid. "Say, do you want to wear my hat? I bet it will fit you perfectly."

"I guess," says Sadness as the Mind Worker places his construction hat on her head.

"Now just stand there *quietly*, okay?" he says.

He plugs the cable into the green port—and there's a spark of energy.

"Whoops," he says, avoiding Sadness's gaze. "Guess that should have gone in the red port."

"I told you," Sadness mumbles.

The Mind Workers continue tinkering with the console. They start to pack up their tools just as the Train of Thought rolls in. That means Riley is waking up.

"Okay, everybody, up and at 'em!" Joy calls as the dream shuts off and Riley starts to open her eyes. "Riley's got a busy day ahead of her at school."

Mind Workers getting off the train begin to unload ideas, facts, and opinions onto the receiving area at Headquarters. The Mind Workers who repaired the console start to board the train. A yellow one yanks Sadness by the arm.

"Come on, no slacking!" he says, pulling Sadness onto the train. Since she's wearing a construction hat, she looks like a Mind Worker!

"But I—" Sadness protests, but it's too late. The engine snorts, and the Train of Thought starts to chug away.

"Oh no. I guess I'm going back to the Mind World," she says.

None of the other Emotions notice. They're too busy getting ready for Riley's day!

If you travel with Sadness to the Mind World, go to page 39.

If you hang out in Headquarters to see what happens there, go to page 77.

(continued from page 76)

The Mind Worker climbs up onto the platform as Sadness is putting the thought back into the Facts crate. He takes it from her hand, reads it, and laughs.

"You think this is a fact? Ha! Whether something is sad is an opinion, not a fact," he says.

"But Riley cried when she read it. So it's sad," Sadness says.

"It's a fact that Riley was sad when she read the book, but not that the book is sad," the Mind Worker corrects her.

"Well, I think it's a gray area," Sadness mumbles.

The Mind Worker jumps off. "Don't come back!" he calls out as the train chugs into motion again.

When the train reaches Headquarters, Sadness climbs down from the platform.

"Oh, hi, Sadness!" says Joy. "What were you doing on that train?"

"Long story," Sadness replies.

Fear rushes up to her. "Riley is trying to make friends with this new girl at school, and everything's going wrong! Do you want to weigh in?"

Sadness is still feeling bad about what the Mind Worker said on the train.

"No, I'd better not," she says. "I'll probably just make things worse."

"Oh, come on, Sadness, you know better than that!" Joy says. "Let us tell you what happened. I'm sure you can help!"

Sadness nods. "Okay . . ."

THE END

(continued from page 108)

"No way am I turning things over to you," says Disgust. She puts an idea into the console. "Watch this."

Riley walks away from her friends and heads into the girls' restroom. She looks in a mirror and takes the elastic band out of her hair.

"What is Riley doing?" Fear asks.

"Haven't you noticed? Madison, Tamika, and Denver are all wearing side braids. Riley should, too," says Disgust.

Riley quickly changes her hair and then walks past the cool-girl table. Madison smiles at her and says hi, and Riley says hi back.

"There's an extra seat," says Denver, pointing to an empty seat next to Madison.

Disgust almost faints with excitement. "It worked!"

Riley sits down and puts her lunch bag on the table. Madison points to the hockey decal on it.

"Are you just a hockey fan, or do you play?" she asks.

"I play for the Foghorns," Riley says. "Why, do you play, too?"

Madison nods. "Ice hockey's pretty big back in Chicago."

"I'm from Minnesota. It's a big deal there, too," Riley says.

Denver rolls her eyes. "Hockey is so boring!"

"But hockey players are not," says Tamika. "Like Dan Chang. Isn't he so cute?"

Anger pounds his fist on the console. "Excuse me! Riley and Madison were talking about hockey! It is *not* boring!"

Denver and Tamika talk about boys for the rest of lunch, so Riley barely gets a chance to talk to Madison. When the bell rings, she passes Alexis and Sam. They both look hurt

because Riley didn't sit with them—but that's something only Sadness would notice. The other Emotions don't see it.

When school ends, Riley is on her way to meet up with Alexis and Sam when she sees Madison standing by herself.

"Riley needs to walk home with Madison," says Disgust.

"No way! I'm tired of chasing after Madison," says Anger.

"Besides, we don't even know where Madison lives. What if we get lost on the way home?" asks Fear.

"It might be fun to walk home with Madison," says Joy. "We could talk some more about hockey."

If Riley walks home with Alexis and Sam, go to page 33.

If Riley walks home with Madison, go to page 116.

(continued from page 127)

Anger doesn't want to see those angry memories lost forever. He races up to the Forgetter pushing the wheelbarrow.

"Don't you know who I am?" he asks. "I'm Anger!"

"Well, you do seem kind of angry," the Forgetter admits.

"I am. Now get those red memories up to Headquarters right away!" Anger demands.

"I told you, I can't do that," the Forgetter says.

"Fine!" fumes Anger. "If you won't, I will!"

Anger grabs as many red memory spheres as his arms will hold. Then he runs to catch up to the Train of Thought.

"Hey, get back here!" Bobby yells.

"You can't do that!" Paula calls after him.

"Yes I can! I'm doing it!" Anger says gleefully.

He outruns the Forgetters and hops on the train back to Headquarters. When he arrives, a yellow sphere pops up through the recall tube and begins playing a cheerful tune.

"Today's gonna be a happy day, a sappy day, a nappy day!"

"Oh, yay!" Joy cries happily. "It's Cheesey, the cartoon mouse!"

"Noooooo!" Anger cries, dropping the memory spheres. "It's that annoying song from that show Riley watched when she was four!" Anger fumes. He's always hated it—and Bobby and Paula must have figured that out.

Smoke pours out of the top of Anger's head. "I never should have gone into the Mind World!"

THE END

(continued from page 84)

Anger takes the controls just as it's Riley's turn to serve. Riley spikes it hard at Sam, and it bounces off her head.

"Hey!" Sam yells.

"Ha! How does *she* like it?" Anger asks.

Coach van Saders sees Riley's spike. He blows a whistle.

"Riley, that was bad sportsmanship," he says.

Riley tries to argue. "But she—"

"You're benched till you cool down," Coach says, ignoring her.

Riley stomps off toward the bleachers.

Disgust looks at Anger and shakes her head. "Nice going."

THE END

(continued from page 119)

Disgust moves closer to the pizza parlor. It looks sort of familiar. She turns to keep walking. There's another pizza parlor in front of her.

"Weird," she mutters.

She turns left, and there's another pizza parlor. Everywhere she turns, there's a pizza parlor!

"I think I know what déjà vu is now," Disgust says.

She walks backward—and accidentally enters the pizza parlor behind her. A girl's voice says, "Your pizza is ready."

Disgust turns. It's broccoli pizza!

"Aaaaaaaaah! Broccoli!" Disgust screams. She runs out of the building as fast as she can.

THE END

"Let me have that!" Anger says, grabbing the controls as Riley answers the phone.

"Hello?" Riley says.

"Riley, where are you?" Sam asks. "Why didn't you walk home with us? You're acting so weird!"

"I am not acting weird!" Riley protests. "I just walked a different way, okay?"

"It's like you're ignoring us," says Sam. "You always pick me or Alexis first when you're team captain."

"Well, I just wanted to do something nice for Madison," says Riley. "I know what it's like to be new at school. But you wouldn't understand that."

"You can be nice without ignoring your real friends," says Sam.

"Oh yeah? Well, my real friends don't call me weird," Riley says, and she hangs up on Sam.

Mom opens the front door. "Riley, what's going on?"

"Nothing," Riley says, stomping up the stairs.

Mom shakes her head. "No stomping, young lady, or I'll take that phone away from you!"

"What is everyone's problem?" Anger fumes. "Sam and Mom just don't understand! Well, who needs them, anyway?"

Fear shakes his head. "I told you we shouldn't have answered the phone!"

THE END

(continued from page 100)

"I don't want to scare Madison off," says Joy. "We'll try talking to her again at lunch."

Later, when the lunch bell rings, Riley hurries to catch up to Madison in the hallway.

"Hey," she says. "It looks like you brought your own lunch. I did, too." Riley holds up her lunch bag.

Madison nods. "You know, I wanted to ask you—"

Riley interrupts her. "So maybe I didn't tell you enough about how great this school is. I left my best friend behind in Minnesota when I came here, but I made new friends."

She nods over to Alexis and Sam, who are sitting at the usual lunch table they share with Riley and some other girls.

A dark cloud crosses Madison's face. "Yeah, well, um, I'll see you later."

She darts off.

"That was rude!" says Disgust.

"Maybe she was just hungry," says Joy. "I'm sure she'll talk to us later."

Riley eats lunch and then heads for the girls' restroom. Inside, she hears someone sobbing. She peeks through one of the stalls and sees Madison.

"Oh no! She's crying! What do we do?" asks Fear.

"Ask Sadness. That's her territory," says Disgust.

Then everyone looks around. For the first time, they realize that Sadness isn't there.

"Where is she?" Joy wonders.

"This is no time to play hide-and-seek," Anger fumes, stomping around looking for her.

Joy turns and looks out the window into the Mind World. "Do you think she's out there again?"

"Again? But Sadness can't do that! Something terrible could happen to Riley! She needs

all of us!" Fear wails. "Somebody has to go get her—"

"I will!" say Joy, Disgust, and Anger.

"—and it won't be me!" Fear says.

"Sadness and I went to the Mind World before. I should go," says Joy.

"Yeah, and you almost got lost in the Memory Dump forever," Anger reminds her. "No way. I'll go."

"If you two are just going to argue, then I might as well go," says Disgust.

Fear sighs. "I'll go if I have to. If Sadness doesn't come back soon, something terrible could happen to Riley!"

If Joy goes to look for Sadness, go to page 60.

If Anger goes to look for Sadness, go to page 125.

If Fear goes to look for Sadness, go to page 55.

If Disgust goes to look for Sadness, go to page 118.

(continued from page 88)

The screenwriter looks disappointed.

"I really should get back to Riley," Sadness says.

"Oh, word down here is that Riley's having a great day," the screenwriter says. "She's even making a new friend."

"Welllll . . . ," Sadness says slowly.

"Come on!" the screenwriter says, and she grabs Sadness by the arm.

They weave their way through the busy studio until they come to a tall, skinny purple Mind Worker.

"This is my friend Gary," says the screenwriter. "Gary, tell her your problem."

"Well, I can never get any big roles," Gary explains. "I'm always an extra. I'm lucky if I get a line! No matter how hard I try, I can't impress the director."

"Wow, that's really sad," says Sadness. "It must feel awful never to be in the spotlight, to always be stuck in the background."

Gary nods. "I've always felt invisible, you know?" he says. "That's why I became an actor. To be noticed. To finally get my moment in the spotlight." He sighs. "Maybe I'm destined to always be ignored." Tears start to flow down his face.

"Gary?"

A Mind Worker with a head of bushy purple hair walks up.

"It's the director," the screenwriter whispers to Sadness.

"Gary, I love what you're doing! The emotion! The passion! You need to star in tonight's dream!"

"Me?" Gary asks, wiping away his tears.

The director pats him on the back. "It's your big break, kid. I'll see you at rehearsal."

As she walks away, Gary smiles at Sadness.

"Thanks for your help!" he says.

"Me? I didn't do anything," Sadness insists.

Go to page 101.

(continued from page 19)

Anger folds his arms across his chest. "You've been calling all the shots today," he tells Disgust. "Give someone else a chance!"

Disgust swings around to face him. "Well, thanks to me, Riley got to eat lunch with Madison!"

Fear looks up at the screen. "Madison is walking away, and Alexis and Sam are walking toward us," he says, and he quickly grabs the empty controls.

Alexis is nervously twirling a strand of hair around her finger. Sam looks mad.

"So we're good enough to walk home with, but not to sit with at lunch?" Sam asks.

"Wh-what do you mean?" Riley stammers.

At the controls, Fear is freaking out. "Sam is mad at us! But why? Why?"

"I'm pretty mad that you ditched us at lunch for the popular table," Sam says.

"I'm not mad, exactly," adds Alexis. "I guess

I'm wondering why you didn't sit with us. I told Sam you probably had a good reason."

"Sam's mad?" Anger fumes. "Shouldn't she be happy for Riley?"

Fear is still at the controls.

"Well, Madison is new, and she waved hi, and then Denver called me over. I was just trying to be nice," Riley says.

"See? She was just trying to be nice," repeats Alexis.

"So you won't sit with them again tomorrow?" Sam asks.

Riley shakes her head. "No way. That was a one-time thing."

Sam relaxes. "Okay then. So what should we do this weekend?"

"I think we should either rate our favorite potato chip flavors or do a marathon of teen vampire movies," says Alexis

"How about both?" Riley says with a grin, and the girls walk home together happily.

"Hey, I did it!" Fear says. "I saved Riley's friendship."

"But Riley's still not friends with Madison," Disgust points out. "We'll have to try again tomorrow!"

THE END

Disgust takes the controls. It's Riley's turn to serve, and she lobs one over the net. When it comes back long, Riley taps it toward Madison.

"Madison, it's yours!" Riley calls out.

Madison hits it over the net, and it falls between two players.

"Nice going!" Riley says as she high-fives her.

For the rest of the game, Riley passes the ball to Madison whenever she can. Across the net, Sam rolls her eyes.

Riley's team wins, and she high-fives Madison again as they head to the locker room. Just then, the Train of Thought pulls up and Joy and Sadness step off.

"How's it going with Madison?" Joy asks.

"Bonding over volleyball," says Disgust. "I'm a genius!"

But Sadness notices that Sam looks mad and Alexis looks worried. Sam walks up to

Riley. "Will you be walking home with us later, or with your *new* friend?" she asks.

"Uh-oh," says Sadness. "It looks like befriending this new girl is upsetting Sam and Alexis."

"Riley didn't mean to upset them," Fear says.

"We can fix it now that you're here," Joy says, slapping Sadness on the back. "I know you can do it! And when that's done, we'll have three good friends in San Francisco!"

THE END

(continued from page 12)

Sadness sighs as the train chugs away from Headquarters, across the vast cavern that leads to the Mind World. A track appears as the train moves along it, and then disappears behind it.

The Mind World is a spectacular sight. Glowing light lines lead from Headquarters to Riley's Islands of Personality. The islands have changed as Riley has grown, since they're based on her core memories, the most important moments in her life. Right now, Riley has several islands humming along: Family, Hockey, Friendship, Goofball, Honesty, Fashion, Boy Band, and Tragic Vampire Romance.

Beyond the islands is a plateau that seems to stretch into infinity. It contains the endless shelves of Long Term Memory, which store Riley's memories. Each memory is a glowing sphere, and the color of the ball is a clue to the memory inside. Yellow memories are happy; blue memories are sad; green memories are gross; red memories are angry; and purple memories are scary. When the Emotions work together, the spheres can even become multicolored, with beautiful swirls of yellow, blue, purple, red, and green.

Also on the plateau are buildings that take care of other parts of Riley's mind, like her Subconscious and her imagination. In Dream Productions, Mind Workers are busy every night creating Riley's dreams.

Sadness gazes at the scene in front of her.

"Uh-oh. The last time I was here, things

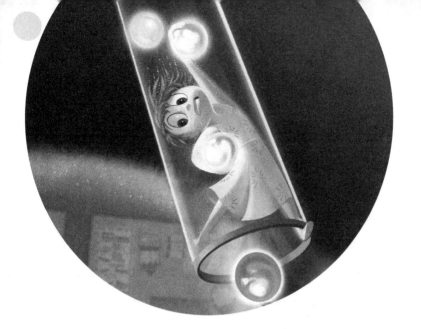

didn't go so well," she says. She's thinking about when she and Joy accidentally got sucked into the Mind World through a memory recall tube. They almost couldn't get back!

The train reaches the first station in the Mind World and screeches to a stop. Sadness tumbles off the platform she's sitting on.

She stands up and sighs. "I should really get on that train and go right back to Headquarters," she says, but when she turns around, the train is already chugging away.

"I'll never run fast enough to catch up to it," she says gloomily.

She is in the stacks of Long Term Memory. Nearby, she sees a Forgetter—a Mind Worker who removes memories that Riley doesn't need anymore and sends them to the Memory Dump. He's skinny and blue and is wearing a white hard hat. He's frowning as he looks down at his clipboard.

Sadness approaches him. "Are you sad? I'm sad, too. I need to get back home and I don't know how."

"I'm lost," says the Forgetter. "It's my first day on the job, and I can't find the memory I'm looking for. Bobby and Paula are going to be so steamed! Can you help me?"

Sadness thinks. She knows a lot about the Long Term Memory shelves. But she might not get it right, and then this new Forgetter will just be even sadder.

If Sadness doesn't help the Forgetter, go to page 56.

If Sadness doesn't help the Forgetter, go to page 56.

If Sadness helps the Forgetter, go to page 93.

Anger turns and sees three red Mind Workers running up to him. They're all wearing T-shirts with his picture on them!

"Back off, freaks!" Anger yells.

One of them laughs. "Classic Anger! Love it. I'm Gus, and this is Barbara and Slim. We're your fan club!"

"My what?" Anger asks.

"Your fan club," says Barbara. "We've seen what you do up there. You're inspiring!"

"Yeah, like not letting that jerk cut in front of Riley on the movie line," says Slim.

"And insisting on a later bedtime for Riley," adds Gus.

"Riley is twelve! She's not a little kid anymore!" Anger says.

"Exactly!" says Gus. "You're amazing. And now you're here in person. What are you doing here, anyway?"

"I'm looking for Sadness," says Anger. "She

came down here and got lost somewhere."

"We'll find her for you," offers Barbara.

"No problem," says Slim. "You can look at this scrapbook of yourself while you wait."

"Well, okay," Anger says. He flips through the scrapbook, and before he knows it, Gus, Barbara, and Slim have brought Sadness to him.

"Hey," says Sadness. "Thanks for coming to find me. Now we can go back and help Riley."

"Go back without me," says Anger. "I owe it to my fan club to spend some time with them."

"Great!" says Gus. "Can you tell us about that time Riley was so mad about getting fouled in a hockey game that she scored three goals?"

"Anything for my fans!" Anger says.

THE END

(continued from page 84)

Fear takes the controls. It's Riley's turn to serve, and she lobs an easy ball over the net. Marcus hits a hard spike, and it slams to the gym floor before anyone on Riley's team can go for it.

"You delivered that serve to them on a silver platter!" Anger yells.

"Well, Riley shouldn't hit it *too* hard. She could hurt herself," Fear explains.

"Our serve!" Marcus yells as the team rotates their lineup. Matt Kim is up next, and he's a monster on the court; he sends the ball spinning over the net right at Riley.

"Aaaah! It's going to hit us in the face!" Fear yells, and Riley jumps out of the way.

"Our point!" Marcus yells. He high-fives Matt.

"Oh, come on!" Anger cries. "This is volleyball, not dodgeball!"

But with Fear at the controls, that's all Riley

does when a ball comes at her—she dodges it. Marcus's team wins easily.

"Well, that was fun," Disgust says sarcastically.

"Here comes Sam," Fear says. "We should tell her good game."

But Riley doesn't have a chance.

"Riley, what was up with that?" Sam asks. "You pick some new girl over me and Alexis?"

Fear starts to stammer. "Oh no! She—she's mad. Wh-what do we do? What do we do?"

But before anyone can answer, he puts an idea in the console. Riley decides to run into the locker room without answering Sam. And after school, when Riley sees Sam and Alexis waiting to walk home with her, she turns and walks in the opposite direction.

"This way, we avoid a fight with Sam," says Fear. "Good strategy, right?"

Disgust shrugs. "I guess. But I need to point out that we are now walking home alone."

When Riley gets home, her cell phone rings.

"It's Sam!" Fear says. "I'm not picking up. No way!"

If Anger answers the call, go to page 24.

If Disgust answers the call, go to page 64.

(continued from page 73)

Dave and Frank start to walk toward Jangles. But Sadness has an idea. She runs to catch up to them.

Jangles spots them. He drops the giant French fry he's holding and looks down. His red nose is enormous. Each one of his teeth is as big as Sadness. Wiry blue hair shoots out from either side of his head.

"Who's the birthday girl?" he asks.

"I am!" Sadness calls out.

Frank nudges her. "Uh, ma'am, I wouldn't say that if I were you."

Jangles's crazy eyes light up. "The birthday girl!"

"That's right!" she says. "But the party's not here. Follow me!"

Sadness turns and runs as fast as she can. She knows that the dark, spooky building holding Riley's Subconscious is up ahead.

"Birthday girl!" Jangles calls after her.

Sadness looks behind her. It's a mistake. Jangles is terrifying. His huge red clown shoes slap the ground loudly as he chases her.

Sadness is puffing and panting. She's not sure she'll make it. Then she spots the long staircase that leads to the Subconscious.

"Down here!" she yells.

She hurries down the stairs and opens the creaky doors to the Subconscious. Jangles is right behind her now.

"The party's inside!" Sadness shouts. She's exhausted. But she needs to make one more tricky move.

She runs inside the dark Subconscious. Jangles follows her. Then she quickly turns and runs between his enormous shoes!

She races back outside and slams the doors behind her. She pushes her body against them. Dave and Frank come running up.

"You did it!" cheers Dave.

"Oh, it was nothing," says Sadness shyly. Then she hears the whistle of the Train of Thought. "Oh no! I've got to go."

"Bye, ma'am!" yells Frank.

"Thanks for saving the day!" Dave calls out.

Sadness gets to the station just as the Train of Thought pulls up. As she rides back to Headquarters, she thinks about what Dave said.

"Did I really save the day?" she wonders out loud. "Yeah, I guess I did."

When she gets back to Headquarters, the other Emotions are all gathered around the console. Disgust is the first to notice her.

"Oh, there you are," she says. "Riley's trying to make friends with this new girl, Madison, and nothing's working."

"Maybe you can help us," suggests Joy.

Sadness smiles. "You know, I think I can!"

THE END

"Aw, come on, give him a chance!" Joy urges Disgust.

"Fine," says Disgust, stepping away from the controls. "Just don't mess this up!"

"I won't. Watch," Anger says.

Riley walks over to the cool-girl table.

"Hi, Madison," she says. "I was wondering if you wanted to sit with me and my friends."

Disgust slaps a hand against her forehead. "Are you kidding me? Right in front of Denver and Tamika? That's crazy!"

Denver glares at Riley. "Um, excuse me, but can't you see that she's sitting with us?"

Anger is trying to keep his cool.

"Yeah," Riley answers. "But it's a free country, right? Madison can sit wherever she wants."

Disgust groans. "Free country? Now Riley sounds like a dork!"

"Just go back to your table, Riley," says Tamika.

Steam starts pouring out of Anger's head. "Is she kidding? She can't tell us what to do!"

"Anger, don't!" Joy yells.

But it's too late.

"You're not the boss of me, Tamika!" Riley says. "You think you're so cool, but that doesn't mean you're better than everybody!"

Then Riley stomps back to her regular lunch table.

Disgust buries her head in her hands. "This is awful! Riley has just started to fit in. This is a big step backward!"

"Look on the bright side," says Joy. "We've still got Alex and Sam."

THE END

As the Train of Thought rolls into Headquarters, Fear jumps onto the platform.

"I've got to get Sadness before something bad happens to Riley!" he wails. "She might be in Long Term Memory . . . but I'd probably just get lost. What if she's in the Subconscious? It's dark and scary there! Maybe she's by the Memory Dump. But I'd probably trip and fall and never come back!"

He jumps off the train before it pulls away. "The most courageous thing I can do is stay here! Riley needs my logical thinking to be safe."

Joy puts an arm around him. "Hang in there, buddy. We'll send someone else when the next train comes."

THE END

"I'll probably just get us more lost," Sadness replies. "Sorry."

She shuffles away, looking down at her tiny feet as she walks. She feels bad about not helping the Forgetter, and even worse about letting Riley down. The last time she and Joy were in the Mind World, Riley almost got into big trouble!

"I just hope I can catch up to that train," she says.

Since Sadness is looking down at her feet, she doesn't pay attention to where she's headed. When she finally looks up, all she sees is ice.

"This isn't a train station," she says with a shiver.

Sadness has arrived at Hockey Island, a land covered with ice, just like a hockey rink. Two towering crossed hockey sticks and a gleaming trophy loom over the buildings on the island:

a rink, a locker room, and an equipment shed.

Sadness takes a step forward and almost slips on the ice.

"I'd better get out of here," she says.

Then she hears saws humming and hammers pounding. Curious, she turns to see a group of Mind Workers busy hanging a new sign over the arena. It's green and reads **FOGHORNS**.

"That's Riley's new ice hockey team," Sadness remarks.

"That's right, lady," says a red Mind Worker. "Out with the Prairie Dogs, in with the Foghorns!"

"Riley was so sad when she had to leave the Prairie Dogs," Sadness remembers.

"Well, that was the old Riley. The new Riley has a new team," snaps the Mind Worker.

Sadness nods. "She loves being on the Foghorns now. But she was really sad when they lost last week."

An orange Mind Worker nods. "I know how that feels. I lost the sack race at the company picnic this year," she says.

"Yeah, but that water-balloon fight afterward cheered you up," says her boss, a red Mind Worker.

"Frozen yogurt always cheers Riley up after a game," Sadness says.

"That's it!" the orange Mind Worker exclaims. "We've been looking to expand. A frozen yogurt stand would be perfect! It's where Riley goes to celebrate when the team wins, and to cheer up when she loses."

The red boss nods. "It's just what we need," he says. He turns to Sadness. "You've got some great ideas, lady. You should go over to Dream Productions. They're having some trouble over there."

"Oh, I'm sure they don't need me," says Sadness. "Besides, I need to look for the Train of Thought."

If Sadness looks for the Train of Thought, go to page 128.

If Sadness goes to Dream Productions, go to page 85.

(continued from page 29)

The Train of Thought pulls into the station, and as Mind Workers unload it, Joy hops on.

"Hey, you can't ride this!" scolds a red Mind Worker.

"It's an emergency! My friend Sadness is down in the Mind World somewhere, and I've got to find her!" Joy says.

The Mind Worker grumbles a bit, but he lets Joy ride the train into the Mind World. She hops off after the train stops at the Long Term Memory shelves.

Joy spots a Forgetter. "Have you seen my friend? She's blue, wears glasses?"

"Yeah, I saw her. She helped me out," says the Forgetter. He points down a row. "She went that way."

"Thanks!" cries Joy, and she runs off down the aisle.

The aisle opens into Imagination Land. Joy and Sadness have visited it before. It contains

some of the coolest things Riley has ever imagined, including a forest of giant French fries and an Imaginary Boyfriend Generator.

"Why would Sadness go there?" Joy wonders.

She walks over to it—and sees Sadness running toward her with Dave and Frank.

"The Subconscious guards?" Joy asks. "What are they doing way out here?"

"Who's the birthday girl?"

An enormous, scary-looking clown is stomping after Sadness and the guards.

"Jangles!" Joy cries. "Why is he still out?"

Jangles hears his name. He smiles when he sees Joy. He reaches down and scoops her up in his giant hand.

"Who's the birthday girl?" he asks.

"Not me!" Joy replies.

"Who's the birthday girl?" Jangles asks again.

"Heeeeelp!" Joy yells.

Sadness skids to a stop. She looks up and sees that Jangles is holding Joy.

"Oh no," she says. "What do we do now?"

If Sadness becomes the birthday girl, go to page 69.

If Sadness has another plan, go to page 111.

If you want to see what's happening back in Headquarters, go to page 82.

(continued from page 49)

Disgust takes the controls. "Let me handle this. I'll smooth it over. Without Sam and Alexis, Riley's back at square one."

"Hello?" Riley says.

"Riley, where are you?" Sam asks. "Why didn't you walk home with us? You're acting so weird!"

"Yeah, sorry, it's been a weird day," Riley says. "I totally meant to tell you I was walking home with Madison, but I forgot. By the way, did I mention how much I like the shoes you wore today?"

"Um, no, but thanks," says Sam. "Did you forget to pick me and Alexis for your team, too?"

"Well, I wanted to do something nice for Madison since she's new. I was going to pick you guys next, I swear, but I didn't have a chance,"

Riley says. "Anyway, you're, like, the best volleyball player in class. You played great today."

Sam is no longer angry. "Yeah, well, thanks."

"So we're okay, right?" Riley asks.

"Yeah, we're okay," Sam says. "Text you later."

In Headquarters, the Train of Thought pulls up and Joy and Sadness hop off.

"Home, safe and sound!" says Joy. "How are things going with Madison?"

Disgust, Fear, and Anger look at one another.

"Well, we don't know, exactly," says Disgust. "We were too busy trying to keep Sam and Alexis from dumping us."

"Good job!" says Joy. "Guess we'll have to try again with Madison tomorrow."

THE END

(continued from page 123)

When Sadness hops off the train at Head-quarters, the other Emotions surround her.

"You're back!" cries Joy.

"I thought you were gone forever!" says Fear.

"What took you so long?" asks Anger.

"Can we please get back to helping Riley?" asks Disgust. "She's been talking to the new girl Madison all day, but Madison doesn't seem to want to be friends."

"Riley has been so nice, but nothing works," says Joy. "And now she just found Madison crying in the girls' restroom. I don't know what's wrong."

"It sounds like she's just sad to be in a new school, like Riley was," says Sadness. She takes the controls. "I can try to help."

Riley leaves the girls' restroom and finds Madison sitting in a corner by herself.

"Hi," she says. "You know, I'm sorry if I said

anything before that upset you. I forgot how sad I was when I first came here from Minnesota. I missed my friends and my old hockey team so much. I even cried in class."

Madison nods. "Yeah, I know the feeling. I was trying not to cry in class earlier."

"So, no pressure," says Riley. "But if you want to sit with me and my friends tomorrow, you should."

"That would be nice," Madison says, giving Riley a small smile.

"Yay!" cheers Joy. "Madison wants to be our friend! We'll be on her team in gym class! And walk home with her from school! And—"

"And what about Alexis and Sam?" asks Sadness. "Doesn't Riley usually do those things with them? Won't they be sad if Riley ignores them?"

"Or mad," says Anger. "We'd be so mad if our friends ignored us."

"I didn't think of that," says Joy. "Gosh, it's good to have you back!"

"Thanks," says Sadness. "It's good to be back."

THE END

"Hey!" Sadness yells. "*I'm* the birthday girl! It's me!"

Jangles looks confused.

"That's right, it's my birthday!" Sadness calls. "And the party can't start until after we all nap. See?"

Sadness lies down and pretends to sleep. Dave and Frank do, too. Jangles yawns. When he opens his hand, Joy falls out. She lands on a cloud drifting by and floats safely to the ground.

Soon Jangles is on the ground, too, snoring peacefully. Sadness and Joy start to tiptoe away.

"Hey!" Dave hisses. "What happens when he wakes up again? How are we supposed to get him back to the Subconscious?"

"I'm sure you'll figure something out," says Joy. She grabs Sadness's hand. "Come on, we've got to get back to Riley!"

Joy starts to run ahead, but Sadness stands
still, like a rock. Joy can't move forward.

"What's wrong?" she asks.

"I feel sorry for Dave and Frank," Sadness
says. "They're not bad guys. And it's kind of our
fault that Jangles got loose in the first place.
You saw him. He stomps around like some kind
of giant monster."

"Giant monster movies are fun," says Joy.

"But I guess not if you're *in* them."

"I think we should help Dave and Frank find a way to get Jangles back to the Subconscious," Sadness says. "But I'm worried about Riley."

"Me too," says Joy. Then she puts an arm around Sadness's shoulder. "Come on, let's go help those guys! I'm sure it won't take long."

"I hope not," says Sadness.

THE END

(continued from page 96)

"You!" Dave yells, pointing at Sadness. "This is your fault!"

"Me?" asks Sadness.

"Yeah," says Dave. "You and your friend let Jangles out of the Subconscious."

"But that was a while ago," says Sadness. "You still haven't caught him?"

"He's been napping in French Fry Forest, but he just woke up," says Dave.

"Jangles is stomping through Imagination Land like Godzilla, squashing French fries under his big clown shoes," says Frank.

"I can see that," says Sadness.

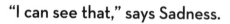

Jangles turns and spots them. "Who's the birthday girl?" he asks again.

"I think he needs to get back into the Subconscious before something bad happens," says Sadness.

"Yeah, we got this, lady," says Frank.

"Um, sure, we got this," says Dave, nervously looking up at Jangles.

Sadness thinks about how she and Joy escaped from Jangles by tricking him. Maybe she can help.

If Sadness helps Dave and Frank, go to page 50.

If Sadness lets Dave and Frank handle it, go to page 109.

(continued from page 88)

Sadness runs as fast as her tiny legs can carry her. She flags down the train, and it pulls to a stop for her. Puffing and panting, she drags herself onto the platform and flops down on her back.

Once she's caught her breath, Sadness sits up and props her back against a crate marked **FACTS**. There are more crates on the platform marked **FACTS** and others marked **OPINIONS**, on their way to Headquarters so that Riley can use them throughout the day.

The train starts up again, moves a few feet, and then comes to a sudden stop.

Thump! Two of the crates topple over. Facts and opinions spill out onto the platform.

Sadness can hear two Mind Workers arguing in the front of the train.

"Why did you stop me?" one asks.

"Why did you make an unauthorized stop?" the other shoots back.

"There's an Emotion stranded out here. I had to."

"What? Again! She'd better not be causing any trouble. . . ."

"Oh, dear," Sadness says. She scrambles to put the facts and opinions back into their crates.

A comet is made of ice, dust, and rock. "Fact," says Sadness.

Comets are more interesting than asteroids. "Opinion."

Sadness is busy sorting the facts and opinions when an angry-looking green Mind Worker stomps up to the platform.

"Hey, you! Are you messing things up?" he barks.

"I'm just cleaning up a little," Sadness says.

She looks at the next thought.

Charlotte's Web *is a really sad book.*

Sadness pauses. Riley had to read that book in school last year. It *was* really sad. Riley even cried when she read it. So it's a fact, right?

If Sadness puts the thought into the Facts crate, go to page 14.

If Sadness puts the thought into the Opinions crate, go to page 121.

(continued from page 12)

Joy, Anger, Disgust, and Fear see the world through Riley's eyes as they watch her get ready for school.

"I'm glad she's wearing the new sneakers today," Disgust says. "The other ones were starting to get holes. So not cute!"

"Riley looks cute no matter what she wears," Joy says cheerfully. "Anyway, her new friends don't care what she looks like."

Riley is approaching a street corner where her two new friends, Alexis and Sam, are waiting for her.

"Thank goodness Riley made new friends," Disgust says. "For, like, the first week of school, she walked all by herself! I thought she was going to be a social outcast."

Fear nods. "Yeah, doomed to walk the halls of school alone forever, like a lonely ghost."

"Everyone in school should want to walk with Riley!" Anger fumes. "Riley is the best!"

"Well, now she has Alexis and Sam," says Joy. "I think they're great. Alexis is so funny, just like Riley. And Sam plays hockey with Riley. It's perfect!"

"Well, they're not the *coolest* girls in school," Disgust says. "But they're cool enough."

When Riley and her friends get to school, Riley sees a girl in the front office with her mom and dad. She has blond hair and is nervously twirling the end of her long side braid.

"I think she's new!" cries Fear.

"It's her first day," says Joy. "Remember Riley's first day and how exciting it was?"

"Exciting? It was terrible!" Anger says. "We weren't ready for a new school."

"It was humiliating. Riley cried in front of everyone," Disgust reminds her. "*Cried!*"

"It was terrifying," Fear remembers. "Riley didn't know her way around yet. There could have been trapdoors. Or hidden spider nests."

The Emotions don't even notice that Sadness isn't with them. Without Sadness, they don't remember how sad Riley felt to be away from Minnesota.

"Jonathan is wearing a red hat and a yellow shirt," Alexis says to Riley as they walk to class. She nods toward a tall, skinny boy. "He looks like a pencil!"

"Oh my gosh, he does!" Riley exclaims, and the three friends giggle.

"He may look like a pencil, but he's a great basketball player," Sam points out.

They enter their classroom and take their seats. Everyone is talking and goofing around before the bell rings. Riley sees the new girl walk up to the door. She stands there in the hall and looks around nervously.

"Oh, look, it's the new girl," says Joy. "We should say something to her!"

Disgust reaches for the controls. "She

looks cool. Let me handle this. Riley could use another friend. Having lots of friends is like social insurance."

"I don't know about insurance, but of course you can never have too many friends!" Joy agrees. "Let's just say hi and make her feel welcome!"

If Disgust takes the controls, go to page 105.

If Joy takes the controls, go to page 98.

(continued from page 63)

"Joy and Sadness are gone," says Anger. "Does this feel familiar to anyone?"

Fear wrings his hands. "Oh, gosh, this didn't work out so well last time."

"Last time was different," Disgust says. "Riley was dealing with a whole big move then. Now we just have to handle a crying girl. It's not such a big deal."

The stall door swings open, and Madison comes out. She's not crying anymore. She dries her eyes and leaves without seeing Riley behind her.

"Whew!" says Fear. "She doesn't know we saw her crying."

"That's good," agrees Disgust. "Now Riley just has to get through a normal school day. Leave it to me."

After lunch Riley has biology, and then gym class with Coach van Saders.

"All right, we're going to play volleyball today.

I need four team cap-tains," Coach says. "Riley, Marcus, Eric, and Olivia."

"Oh, gosh. Riley's captain? What if she picks a terrible team? What if they lose?" Fear worries.

"Riley's going to pick a great team," Disgust says. "Starting with Madison."

"But Riley always picks Sam first," says Fear.

"It's not a problem," Disgust says. "She's just trying to make Madison feel welcome, right?"

"I'll take Madison," Riley says. Sam nudges Alexis and starts whispering. Then Marcus picks Sam, and Coach van Saders pits Riley's team against Marcus's.

"I'll serve!" Sam yells across the net. She spikes it really hard, right at Riley, and the ball hits Riley in the arm.

"Hey!" Riley says.

"Sorry. That was an accident," Sam says, but she doesn't sound sorry.

"What was that?" Anger asks. "She did that on purpose!"

"I think she's mad that Riley didn't pick her first," says Fear.

"Whatever. Let her be mad," says Disgust. "Madison looked happy when Riley picked her for the team."

"Sure, but if Sam's mad now, then Riley's just getting one friend and losing another," Fear points out. "I think we're messing up again."

"Speak for yourself!" snaps Disgust.

"Watch the ball!" Anger yells as Riley misses an easy lob. "Come on, people, let's get our act together!"

If Anger takes the controls, go to page 22.

If Disgust takes the controls, go to page 37.

If Fear takes the controls, go to page 46.

The orange Mind Worker frowns. "Oh, too bad. I know our friends there could use some help."

Sadness feels bad for the Mind Worker. "Well, I guess I could walk toward Dream Productions while I go look for the train. . . ."

"Thanks!" says the Mind Worker boss. Then he turns back to his crew. "Let's get cracking on that new yogurt shop!"

Sadness sighs and walks away from Hockey Island toward Dream Productions. She knows the way. When she and Joy were here, Joy wanted to wake Riley up to get the Train of Thought running again. Joy thought a super-happy dream would wake Riley up. But things didn't exactly go as planned.

"I don't even know why I'm going here," Sadness says. "Whatever's happening in Dream Productions, I'm sure I'll just make it worse."

Soon she passes through the golden

archway leading into Dream Productions. It's a sprawling movie studio. Mind Workers are busy running around, preparing for Riley's dreams that night. Prop masters are rummaging through crates of random objects. Costumers are sewing and ironing. Actors are practicing their lines. Nobody even notices Sadness.

"Why did I come here?" Sadness wonders aloud. "Everything looks fine."

Then she spots a green Mind Worker with curly hair and glasses. She's leaning against a wall, holding her laptop. She looks sad.

Sadness walks up to her. "Hi," she says.

"Have you ever had writer's block?" the Mind Worker blurts out.

"What do you mean?" asks Sadness.

"I'm supposed to be writing a big dream for Riley tonight," the screenwriter explains. "But I'm out of ideas! The director says we've got to lay off the Rainbow Unicorn dreams. She wants something *deep*. What does that even mean?"

"Well, I know that Riley has deep thoughts sometimes," Sadness replies. "When she lived in Minnesota, she used to go to the ice pond and stare at the ice and think. Do you ever do that?"

The Mind Worker looks reflective. "Well, there's no ice pond around here, but sometimes I go to French Fry Forest and look up at the French fries. They're so tall and majestic! And I think, wow, if Riley's imagination can create that, what else can it create?" She snaps out of her memory and looks at Sadness. "That's deep! I get it now. Thanks for your help. Hey, you should meet my friend Gary. He could use a little inspiration, too."

Toot-toot! Sadness hears the Train of Thought getting closer.

She frowns. "Well, I really have to be going. . . ."

If Sadness meets Gary, go to page 30.

If Sadness runs after the Train of Thought, go to page 74.

(continued from page 100)

Fear takes the controls. "I can't wait to share all the data I've collected with Madison."

When class is over, Riley rushes after Madison.

"Hey!" Riley says. "I know you must have a lot of questions on your first day, but you should know that the school is pretty safe. Like, for example, there are no giant spiders in the bathroom. And there have been no cases of food poisoning from the school cafeteria. Timmy D'Angelo threw up that one time, but it was a virus. And there were only three kids who got hurt in gym class last year. And—"

"Uh, okay, thanks," Madison interrupts her. She rushes off, looking spooked.

Fear smiles. "That went well! I think she got it. She's a smart kid."

THE END

Disgust walks past the pizza parlor.

"That's weird. *Déjà vu* sounds French, but pizza is Italian," she remarks.

"*. . . pizza is Italian.*"

Her own voice echoes back at her through the fog.

"Hello?" she calls.

"*Hello?*"

The fog clears, and Disgust sees a small army of . . . other Disgusts! There are copies of her everywhere! One is jumping off the Train of Thought. Another is walking past the pizza parlor. Yet another is waking up and yawning.

She grins. "Now I know what déjà vu is. It's seeing me over and over again! It's the perfect place!"

She stares at the copies of herself, transfixed. She could stay there all day.

Then she notices something. In the scene where she's walking, Sadness is behind her. She's putting on her glasses.

"Sadness!" she yells. "I'd better go find her."

She sighs. "Bye, me! I'll miss you."

Disgust tears herself away from Déjà Vu and walks to the nearest building—Dream Productions. She spots Sadness outside, surrounded by Mind Workers.

"Can you help me rewrite this scene?" one Mind Worker asks her as others gather around.

"I'd like to help, but I need to get back to Riley," Sadness says.

They're hounding Sadness like paparazzi.

Disgust marches up. "Back off! My friend has important places to be," she says. She pulls Sadness away.

"Thanks," Sadness says. "Everybody wanted my help. I didn't want to hurt their feelings."

"It's a good thing I showed up, because Riley

needs our help," Disgust says. "There's a new kid in school, and Riley can't make friends with her. She likes hockey. But she might be too cool for Riley. Although she keeps frowning, and she even cried."

"She just sounds sad," says Sadness.

"See! That's why we need you. You're good with that stuff," says Disgust.

On the train ride back to Headquarters, Disgust and Sadness come up with a plan to befriend Madison.

"You know, we make a pretty good team," says Disgust.

"Thanks," says Sadness.

"Since we're going to be hanging out together, can I give you a makeover?" Disgust asks.

Sadness sighs. "Oh, dear."

THE END

The Forgetter looks worried and sad.

"What memory are you supposed to find?" Sadness asks.

He looks down at his clipboard. "Riley, age four and three months. Riley watches ants carry a cheese puff back to their anthill. I looked in age four, section B for *bugs*, but it's not there!"

"Well, that's a good start," says Sadness. "But I've read all the Mind Manuals. I think you might want to look in section I."

"Section I?" the Forgetter asks.

"For *insects*," says Sadness.

He slaps his forehead. "Of course! Let me try there. Will you come with me? Please?"

Sadness follows the young Forgetter through the long, winding aisles to section I. He looks at all the memories and frowns.

"What are all these subsections?" he asks.

"Well, ants have six legs, so you might want

to try 6L," Sadness suggests to him.

"6L! Got it!" says the Forgetter.

They find 6L, which still contains rows and rows of memories.

"These are sub-subsections!" groans the Forgetter.

"I think you might need sub-subsection CU," says Sadness. "That's for curious memories."

"As opposed to what?" the Forgetter asks.

"Fearful memories. Or educational memories. Or creative memories," Sadness explains. "It helps if you know the memory. Riley wasn't afraid of the ant. She didn't learn about it in preschool or make an ant project in art class. She was just curious about it."

They walk along the aisle and come to a stop. Sadness pulls out a yellow memory sphere that's glowing faintly. Inside, she can see the ants carrying the cheese puff. She hands it to the Forgetter.

"This is great!" he says. "Bobby and Paula will be impressed."

"Well, I should go now," Sadness says. "I have to get back to Riley."

Sadness walks down to the end of the long aisle. She emerges in front of Imagination Land. It's a fun, colorful place fueled by Riley's imagination. There's French Fry Forest, Cloud Town, and even an Imaginary Boyfriend Generator.

Sadness hears screaming.

"He's awake! Jangles is awake!"

Two Mind Workers come running toward Sadness. One is round and blue, and the other is purple with a bushy mustache. Sadness realizes that they are Dave and Frank, the guards from Riley's Subconscious.

Behind them is a giant, terrifying clown. It's Jangles! He scared Riley once at a party, and he's been lurking in her Subconscious ever since.

"Who's the birthday girl?" Jangles bellows.

Go to page 72.

(continued from page 81)

"The best way to make a new friend is to be nice and friendly," says Joy. "That's right up my alley!"

Riley walks up to the new girl, who is still standing by the front door.

"Hi!" Riley says. "I'm Riley. It's your first day here, right? I was new here, too, this year. You'll really like this school. The teachers are nice, and the cafeteria's pretty good. Every Wednesday is spaghetti and meatballs."

"Um, yeah, sounds nice," the new girl says, giving Riley a weird look. Then she walks right past her and finds a seat.

"Great job," says Disgust dryly. "She's our new best friend."

"I don't understand," Joy says. "Riley was super nice and friendly. And who doesn't smile when you talk about spaghetti and meatballs?"

"Maybe she's gluten intolerant," says Fear.

"She must be distracted by all the new kids she's meeting," Joy says. "Or tired, because she was so excited about her first day of school that she got up early. Or maybe she just didn't eat a good breakfast. Riley had oatmeal and a yogurt smoothie, so she always has lots of good energy in the morning. Maybe the new girl ate a donut. Riley should tell her to improve her breakfast strategy."

"Yeah, because that's a *great* way to make new friends," Disgust says sarcastically.

In the classroom, the teacher is introducing the new girl to the class. Her name is Madison, and she's from Chicago.

"I think I know the problem," says Fear. "I think Madison is afraid of being a new kid in a new place. Riley was pretty scared on her first day here. Maybe she could talk about that stuff with Madison. They have a lot in common."

"Madison doesn't want to talk about being scared," says Joy. "That's not fun."

"Well, Riley can't talk again until class is over anyway," Disgust points out.

If Fear takes over the controls, go to page 89.

If Joy stays with the controls, go to page 26.

"I'd better get to rehearsal," Gary says. "It's getting close to Riley's bedtime."

"Already?" Sadness asks. "Oh no! I need to catch the Train of Thought before it stops running."

"I'll go with you," the screenwriter offers. "It's the least I can do."

The screenwriter leads Sadness out of Dream Productions. They head for the nearest train station. When they get there, they see the construction workers from Hockey Island.

"What are you guys doing here?" Sadness asks.

"We were hoping we would catch you on your way back to Headquarters," says the boss. "The frozen yogurt shop is turning out great. Thanks for the idea."

"She helped me with an idea for a new script," says the screenwriter. "She's a real problem solver!"

"I am?" Sadness asks.

"You sure are!" says the construction boss.

Toot-toot! The Train of Thought chugs into the station.

"There's your ride," the screenwriter says. "Come back and visit us sometime."

Sadness climbs aboard the train.

"Bye," she says. "I'll miss you guys."

The train leaves the station and takes Sadness back to Headquarters. When she hops off, the other Emotions surround her. They are frantic.

"Sadness! It's so good to see you!" Joy cries, giving her a hug.

"Where the heck have you been?" asks Anger. "Riley's day got all messed up, and you weren't here to help!"

"Oh no! What happened?" Sadness asks.

"It's a social disaster," replies Disgust. "There was a new girl in school and Riley tried

to be friends with her, but she's, like, not interested, and now Alexis and Sam are mad at her."

Sadness nods. "That's too bad," she says.

"I thought you were gone forever. We can't do this without you!" cries Fear.

"We just can't figure out why Madison doesn't like Riley," Joy explains. "Maybe you can understand her better than we can."

Sadness thinks about all the Mind Workers at the train station, and how they said she helped them.

"Well, I'm here now," she says. "Maybe we can fix things for Riley tomorrow."

THE END

(continued from page 81)

Disgust grabs the controls. "We can say hi and work on keeping Riley from being a social misfit at the same time," she says. "It's a win-win situation. Just watch."

Riley walks up to the new girl. She starts to smile when she sees Riley.

Riley nods. "Hey," she says. Then she turns and walks back to her seat.

"What was that?" Anger yells.

"We're playing it cool," Disgust answers. "We have to make sure this new girl knows we exist. But we can't act like we want to be her friend."

"But we *do* want to be her friend," Joy points out.

"Yes, but if we let her know that, she'll think we're desperate," Disgust says, and rolls her eyes. "Don't you guys know anything?"

The bell rings.

"Fire! Find the nearest exit!" Fear yells.

"It's just the start of class," says Joy. "Shhh. The teacher's going to introduce the new girl."

Riley's teacher smiles at the new girl. "Class, I'd like you to welcome Madison. This is her first day. She moved here all the way from Chicago."

"Hey, that's not too far from Minnesota," Joy says. "Looks like Riley and Madison have something in common."

Disgust is studying the new girl carefully. "Hmm. Big-city girl. That would explain the skinny jeans and the Le Fevre backpack. Very chic. Okay, we've got to step things up."

"Hey, pay attention! You don't want Riley to fail out of school, do you?" Fear asks.

The Emotions watch Riley closely all through class. When the bell rings, Madison hurries out. Riley walks between Alexis and Sam.

"Did you talk to the new girl? What's she like?" Alexis asks.

Riley shrugs. "I don't know."

"She looks cool," remarks Sam. "She'll probably end up being friends with Denver and Tamika."

"Denver and Tamika are *the* coolest girls in the whole school," Disgust reminds the others in Headquarters. "But there's no reason Madison can't be friends with Riley. We'll make our move in the cafeteria and invite Madison to sit with us."

When lunchtime comes, Riley looks for Madison. She finds her—and sees that Denver and Tamika are already sweeping her away to their table!

"Oh no!" Disgust wails. "How did this happen?"

"Who do they think they are, hogging Madison like that?" Anger demands. "Move over. I'm going to handle this now."

"No way!" Disgust protests. "You'll just make

Riley scream and get into an argument."

"I've got a new approach," Anger assures her. "I took an anger management class. Come on, let me try."

If Anger takes over the controls, go to page 53.

If Disgust stays with the controls, go to page 16.

Dave and Frank march toward Jangles.

"Stop right where you are!" yells Dave.

"You're a troublemaker!" calls Frank. "And troublemakers need to be locked up."

Jangles looks down at Dave and Frank. His wild blue hair is sticking out on either side of his head. He's got a huge red nose and a wide clown mouth. Each tooth is as big as one of the Mind Workers.

"TWO birthday girls!" cries Jangles. He picks up Dave in one gloved hand and Frank in the other.

"Put us down right now!" Dave yells.

"Yeah, by order of . . . of us!" adds Frank.

"Are you sure you don't need my help?" Sadness calls up.

"I said we got this!" Frank replies.

"Um, we do?" asks Dave.

Then Sadness hears the toot of the Train of Thought. She knows she needs to get back to

Riley. She hurries to catch the train.

"I'm not sure Dave and Frank will get Jangles locked up," she says. "But Riley might need me!"

THE END

Sadness has an idea—a big one. She turns to the guards.

"Dave and Frank, get all the candy and balloons you can carry," she says. "Confetti, too, if you can find it."

Dave lifts his cap to scratch his head. "Do you really think it's a good time to have a party?"

"I just need you to trust me," Sadness says. "When you get the party supplies, use them to make a trail from Imagination Land to the Subconscious, okay?"

Frank nods. "Yeah, that's pretty smart. But how will we get Jangles back to sleep once he's there? If we don't, he'll just bust out again."

"Just do it," says Sadness. "I'll meet you there, okay?"

"Got it!" say the two guards. They run off.

Sadness looks up at Joy. She's staring right at the clown's big red nose.

"Who's the birthday girl?" he asks.

"I keep telling you, it's not me!" cries Joy.

"Hang in there, Joy!" Sadness calls. Then she, too, disappears.

Dave and Frank come back to Imagination Land a few minutes later and start to leave a trail of candy, balloons, and confetti leading to the Subconscious. The clown's eyes light up when he sees them.

"It's party time!" he shouts, and starts to walk along the trail, picking up candy as he goes.

The trail leads down a long staircase to the big doors of the spooky building that houses Riley's Subconscious. Still holding Joy, Jangles stomps inside.

"No more candy!" Jangles cries.

Dave and Frank are sweating.

"Where is that blue lady?" Dave asks.

"Right here," Sadness says, running up to them. "And I brought some help."

Behind her are the five boys from Boy Band Island!

Jangles pokes his head out the door. "More candy!"

"Now, boys!" says Sadness.

The boys burst into a lullaby in perfect five-part harmony. Jangles starts to yawn. His eyes begin to droop. He sinks to the ground. His hand opens up, and Joy runs out.

"Close the door!" Sadness cries, and Dave and Frank run and shut it just as the lullaby ends.

"Thanks," Dave says.

"You guys, too," Frank says to the band. "That was beautiful."

"You're welcome!" the boy band sings back.

Joy hugs Sadness. "You saved the day!" she says. "Now we have to go help Riley."

On the Train of Thought back to Headquarters, Joy tells Sadness all about the new girl.

"Riley's been telling Madison how great the new school is, and how she'll make friends and everything, but she made Madison cry," Joy explains. "We can't figure it out."

"I think I can," says Sadness. "It's like when Riley first moved here and she missed Minnesota so bad. Riley needed to be sad for a while. I think Madison does, too."

They get back just as school is ending.

"There's Madison!" says Joy. "Riley should walk home with her."

"Okay, but she should tell Alexis and Sam first," says Sadness. "She might hurt their feelings otherwise."

Riley tells Alexis and Sam that she's going to see if Madison wants to walk home with her, and they're cool with it. Then Riley races to catch up to Madison. Sadness is at the controls.

"Hey!" she says, but Madison doesn't look too happy to see her. "Listen, I just wanted to say I'm sorry if the stuff I said before upset you. When I was new here, everyone kept trying to tell me how happy I should be. But I wasn't. I was sad. It's okay if you feel sad, too."

Madison's eyes fill with tears. "Thanks," she says. "Hey, do you want to walk home together? I want to ask you about the hockey team."

"Sure," says Riley.

Joy high-fives Sadness.

"We did it!" Joy cries.

THE END

(continued from page 19)

With Disgust at the controls, Riley calls Madison's name. Madison's head turns as Riley runs toward her.

The two girls start walking together.

"So, you played hockey in Chicago?" Riley asks.

Madison nods. "On the Penguins. All of my best friends were on that team. We practiced all the time, and we'd go skating on the lake for fun. It doesn't get cold enough out here in the winter to skate outside, does it?"

"No," Riley answers. "But the indoor rinks are nice."

"Indoor rinks just aren't the same," Madison says with a sigh. Then she looks at her feet.

That's when the Train of Thought pulls in and Sadness jumps out. The others didn't even realize she was gone.

"Who is that sad girl with Riley?" she asks.

"Were you off reading Mind Manuals again?

That's Madison, the new girl, but she's not sad," says Joy. "She's just quiet."

"She sure looks sad," says Sadness. "What were she and Riley talking about?"

"Hockey. Madison's from Chicago, and she used to play hockey there with her friends," Joy replies.

Sadness nods. "Here, let me try."

She takes the controls. Riley turns to Madison.

"I know how tough it is to leave your old friends behind," Riley says. "I was sad when I first moved here, too. I thought I would miss the snow and my house and my friends. And I do. But I made some new friends. You should meet them. You'll like them."

Madison smiles a little. "I'd like that."

Anger turns to Sadness. "Why didn't you do this before?" he asks.

Sadness sighs. "It's a long story."

THE END

(continued from page 29)

"If we don't get Sadness back here, Riley will have no chance of making friends with Madison," says Disgust. "I can handle myself in the Mind World. I'm going."

When the Train of Thought pulls in, she hops aboard.

"I'll take a sparkling water and a bag of almonds," she announces. Then she looks for a seat—but there are none, just some crates.

"This train needs a serious upgrade," she says with a sniff, sitting on a crate. Then she sees her reflection in a piece of shiny metal.

"Wow, my hair is amazing today," she says.

She's distracted, so she doesn't notice the train's first stop—or the second. When she looks up from her reflection, the train is in front of a building she hasn't seen before.

Disgust hops off the train. "Might as well start here."

Above the building there's a sign that reads

DÉJÀ VU. That's the weird feeling Riley gets when she feels like she's been somewhere or done something before and she's doing it over again.

"'Déjà vu,'" Disgust reads. "Sounds French. Ooh, maybe it's a boutique!"

She opens the door and walks inside, into what appears to be a light fog. She shivers. She takes a few steps, and through the fog she can see . . . a pizza parlor?

"That's funny," Disgust says. "I feel like I've seen that pizza parlor before."

She thinks. "Oh, that's the pizza parlor that Riley went to when she first moved to San Francisco!"

If Disgust explores the pizza parlor, go to page 23.

If Disgust keeps walking, go to page 90.

The Mind Worker climbs onto the platform as Sadness puts the thought in the Opinions crate. He grabs it from her hand.

"'*Charlotte's Web* is a really sad book,'" he reads aloud. "Yup. That's an opinion, all right."

"I know," says Sadness. "Even though Riley got really sad when she read it." She starts to sniffle. "Oh, that poor spider!"

"Well, looks like you've done a pretty good job of sorting things out here," the Mind Worker says. He looks at the fallen thoughts scattered everywhere. "What exactly happened?"

"The train stopped short, and some of the boxes opened," Sadness answers. "It wasn't my fault."

"Of course not," says the Mind Worker. "Here, I'll help you put away the rest."

Sadness and the Mind Worker work together quickly to get the remaining facts and opinions sorted out. Then the Mind Worker picks something up. "Hey, this isn't a fact *or* an opinion," he says.

He holds up what looks like a flowy ribbon. Clouds are moving across it, along with some mixed-up words.

Canada the peacefully sky across goose a like floating

"It's a daydream," the Mind Worker continues. "But it got all mixed up. What does it mean?"

"I don't know," Sadness replies. "Riley has never been to Canada, although it's not far from Minnesota. They were supposed to go one winter to see a hockey game, but then Mom got the flu. Riley was so sad."

"It doesn't say anything here about hockey," says the Mind Worker. "Just some goose."

"Maybe it's a Canada goose," says Sadness. "You know, those big geese you see everywhere. Riley's dad told her they're called

Canada geese, and she thinks about Canada and hockey whenever she sees one."

Sadness looks at the daydream. "Maybe it's this," she says, touching the words and moving them around.

Flying peacefully across the sky like a Canada goose.

When she finishes, the daydream sparkles and flies into a crate marked **DAYDREAMS**.

"You did it!" says the Mind Worker. "Good work! They must be lost without you up in Headquarters. We'd better get you back there."

"Oh, I bet they didn't even miss me," says Sadness, but she can't help smiling at the Mind Worker's compliment.

The Mind Worker scrambles off the platform, and soon the train starts moving again.

Go to page 66.

"Here's what's gonna happen. I'm jumping on that train, I'm getting Sadness, and I'm bringing her back. End of story," Anger says. He climbs onto the Train of Thought after it pulls into Headquarters.

"You can't ride this," a yellow Mind Worker tells him. "You're not an authorized passenger."

"Want to see my credentials?" Anger asks. He holds up a fist. "Here's all the authority I need."

The yellow Mind Worker backs up. "Okay, mister, just don't tell my boss I let you on the train," he says, and then he scurries to another car.

Anger rides the train into the Mind World and jumps off at the first stop, by the Long Term Memory shelves. He sees two Forgetters, Paula and Bobby.

"You two!" he yells. "My friend Sadness came down here. Have you seen her?"

"Maybe we have," says Bobby.

"But you forgot to say the magic word," adds Paula.

"I'll give you a magic word. How about, 'Tell me now'?" Anger asks.

Paula frowns. "No, I said magic word, not words. And those words aren't it."

Then Anger notices something. Another Forgetter is pushing a wheelbarrow of memory spheres toward the Memory Dump. And most of them are red!

"What are you doing with those?" he asks. "Those are great angry memories! You can't dump them!"

The Forgetter shrugs. "Following orders."

Anger starts to run after him when he hears voices behind him.

"Anger! Anger! We're your biggest fans!"

If Anger tries to rescue the red memories, go to page 20.

If Anger stops to talk to his fans, go to page 44.

(continued from page 59)

Sadness walks to the nearest train station and takes the Train of Thought back to Headquarters. When she gets there, the other Emotions are seeing the halls of the school through Riley's eyes.

"Hi, everyone," says Sadness. "Were you worried about me? I accidentally went to the Mind World again."

Disgust turns around. "Oh, were you gone? Sorry, we're all pretty busy here. There's a new girl in school."

"No one even noticed," Sadness says with a sigh. "Oh, well. At least I got back before something bad happened to Riley!"

THE END